Littlest Pet Shop

Sleeping Beauty

By Jessie Pickles
illustrated by Jim Talbot

SCHOLASTIC INC.
New York   Toronto   London   Auckland   Sydney
Mexico City   New Delhi   Hong Kong   Buenos Aires

This book belongs to

Abigail Korus

No part of this publication may be reproduced in whole or in part, stored in a retrieval system,
or transmitted in any form or by any means, electronic, mechanical, photocopying, recording, or otherwise,
without written permission of the publisher. For information regarding permission, write to Scholastic Inc.,
Attention: Permissions Department, 557 Broadway, New York, NY 10012.

ISBN-13: 978-0-545-07905-1
ISBN-10: 0-545-07905-5

Littlest Pet Shop © 2009 Hasbro.
LITTLEST PET SHOP and all related characters and elements are trademarks of and © Hasbro. All Rights Reserved.

Published by Scholastic Inc. SCHOLASTIC and associated logos are trademarks and/or
registered trademarks of Scholastic Inc.

12 11 10 9 8 7 6 5 4   10 11 12 13 14/0

Printed in the U.S.A.   23
First printing, January 2009

Once upon a time, there lived a beautiful princess. With a bit of yarn to bat about and a sweet melody to meow, she was a very happy cat.

The pink princess's three fairy godmothers adored her and her playful ways. They gave her balls of yarn and taught her songs to sing.

However, the frowning fairy was not so playful. The mere sight of delight made her tail feathers twitch.

One day, the king and queen invited the entire kingdom to the pink princess's birthday party. The princess had never seen so many gifts or so many beautiful balls of yarn!

Everyone had a terrific time, except for the frowning fairy. The more the princess played, the more furious the fairy became. In a jealous rage, she cast a curse on the pink princess.

"Sleep forever from the day
a ball of yarn tempts you to play.
Nothing can wake you after that—
except the kiss from a princely cat."

The fairy godmothers heard these wicked words.
They fluttered over to the king and queen to warn them.

Faster than the flick of a tail,
the king and queen banished all balls
of yarn from the land!

The princess was crushed. Being in the castle was no fun at all without balls of yarn to chase after. She wandered out of the castle and into the forest. She tried to cheer herself by purring her favorite song.

Just then, a charming cat came gliding by. *Who is purring that perfect tune?* he thought.

He crept into the clearing and saw the princess singing in a patch of sunshine. Excitedly, he ran over to meet her.

Back at the castle, the king and queen were panicked! *Where is the princess? Has she been catnapped by the frowning fairy?* Without wasting a moment, her fairy godmothers flew out to find her.

Meanwhile, the pink princess and her new friend were happily playing chase. Suddenly, the princess heard the birdcalls of her fairy godmothers. She knew she had to get home right away. She dashed toward the castle, but took one last glance back at the charming cat. As she ran, she realized her mistake—she had never found out the cat's name!

The queen was too worried about the princess to let her roam around. The frowning fairy could trick her with a ball of yarn and send her to sleep forever! And so the pink princess was made to stay inside.

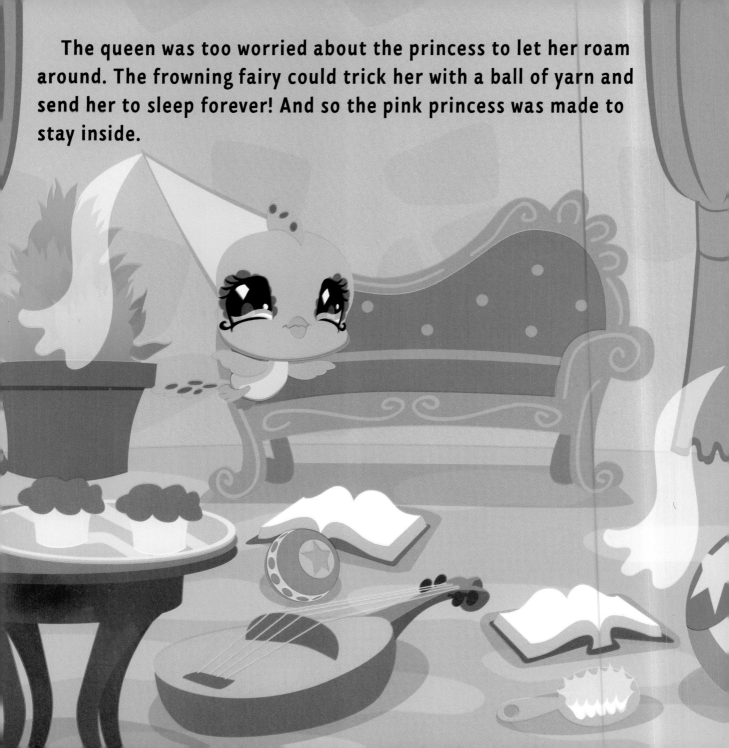

Her fairy godmothers tried to lift her spirits, but nothing worked. Finally, they flew off for a birdbath and left the princess to take a catnap.

As the princess went to lie down, something caught her eye.
It was a string of yarn! The princess couldn't believe her good luck.

She followed the string up a winding staircase . . . all the way to the very top of an old, empty tower.

But the tower wasn't *completely* empty.

Inside was the biggest, most beautiful ball of yarn the pink princess had ever seen! She playfully pounced . . . and in the blink of an eye, she was fast asleep.

When the fairy godmothers returned to the princess's room, they saw the string of yarn—but no princess! They found the princess in the tower, but nothing they did could wake her. With tearful tweets, they put her in bed and sang her favorite song.

Far below, the charming cat wandered around the castle grounds. He wondered if he would ever see the pretty pink kitten again. Suddenly, he pricked up his ears.

He heard a faint, familiar tune coming from the tower. It was the same song that the pretty pink kitten had been singing! He chased the music up the spiraling staircase . . . and found the pink kitten in a deep sleep!

The fairy godmothers explained the evil curse to the worried visitor. Gently, he leaned over to kiss the sleeping beauty.

The princess's eyes fluttered open. The charming cat was a prince—
and his kiss had broken the spell!

The entire kingdom rejoiced! From that day on, the pink princess and her prince lived a long happy life together full of music and big beautiful balls of yarn.